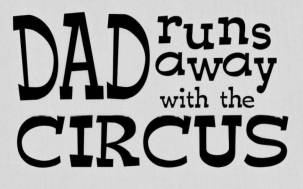

DAD runs away with the CIRCUS

DAD.

CIR

CANDLEWICK PRESS
CAMBRIDGE, MASSACHUSETTS

runs away with the cus

Etgar Keret   illustrated by Rutu Modan

"You'll never guess what's going to happen!"
Dad yelled, swinging from the chandelier.

Audrey and I were still half-asleep, so we didn't even try.

"The circus is in town!" Dad roared.
"And we're all going to see it!"

Dad was so happy. We tried to be happy too, but mostly we were wondering whether he had woken up the neighbors.

That morning, Dad couldn't stop talking about the circus.

He behaved very irresponsibly, pulling all sorts of wild and dangerous stunts that could have ended in tears.

When Mom got home from work, we ironed our best clothes and got ready to drive to the circus.

Audrey had to miss her judo lesson, and I really wanted to watch TV, but we knew that Dad would be insulted if we didn't come along.

It rained all the way to the circus, but Dad didn't pay any attention.

According to Mom, getting soaked could be hazardous to your health. But Dad said that if you compared it to putting your head in a lion's mouth, it was child's play.

The circus tent was huge. Before the lights went down,
we noticed that very few people were there.

The acts were decent, especially the lions and the acrobats. Somehow, though, the way Dad told it had all sounded a little more exciting.

But Dad was having a ball. During the parts he thought were scary, he insisted on covering our eyes.

Audrey whispered to me that this behavior was part of what some people call the generation gap.

After the show, while Audrey and I waited in the car,
Mom and Dad had an argument.

A little later, Mom came back alone and told us that
Dad had decided to run off and join the circus.

Audrey and I told each other it was wonderful that Dad was making such good progress and doing so well.

But deep down, we just wanted him to come home.

And home he came . . .

with the circus!

We all got ready to see the show again, but this time it was really exciting.

This time it was our father who was performing!

But what he did after the show was the best part.
Dad came home with us! On the way, Mom and
Audrey and I told him how great all the different acts

had looked from where we were sitting. Dad hugged
us tight and promised never to run away again.

And from then on, everything went back to being the same as it always had been.

Well, almost the same.

For Orit, the queen of cartwheels
R. M.

Text copyright © 2000, 2004 by Etgar Keret
Illustrations copyright © 2000, 2004 by Rutu Modan
Original Hebrew text translated by Noah Stollman

First U.S. edition 2004

Library of Congress Cataloging-Publication-Data

Keret, Etgar.
Dad runs away with the circus / Etgar Keret ; illustrated by Rutu Modan. — 1st U.S. ed.
p. cm.
Summary: A wildly enthusiastic father surprises his
family when he runs off to join the circus.
ISBN 0-7636-2247-8
[1. Circus — Fiction. 2. Fathers — Fiction.] I. Modan, Rutu, ill. II. Title.
PZ7K4686Dad 2004
[E] — dc22   2003069673

2 4 6 8 10 9 7 5 3 1

Printed in China

This book was typeset in Beniolo and Clichee.
The illustrations were done in pencil,
then digitally layered and colored.

Candlewick Press
2067 Massachusetts Avenue
Cambridge, Massachusetts 02140

visit us at www.candlewick.com